# ADVENTURES OF LITTLE BIRD

## Pirate Dreams

Written and Illustrated by

# JOHNATHAN HILLSTRAND

PEANUT BUTTER PUBLISHING

Seattle, Washington
Portland, Oregon
Denver, Colorado
Vancouver, B.C.
Scottsdale, Arizona
Minneapolis, Minnesota

This book is dedicated to my grandma, mom and dad, my brothers, my son and daughter, my two beautiful grandkids...and the baby bull that sent me to the hospital and the lady who gave me the colored pencils and note pad... without whom this book would have never been created. It is also dedicated to anyone who has a dream and is not afraid to chase it, even against all odds.

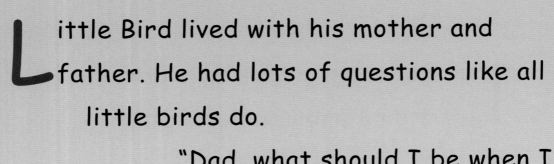

Little Bird lived with his mother and father. He had lots of questions like all little birds do.

"Dad, what should I be when I grow up?" "Son, you can be whatever you want to be."

"Mom, can I be the President of the United

States?" "Yes, Little Bird."

"Mom, can I be a policeman?"

"Yes, Little Bird; you can be a policeman."

"Mom, can I be a fireman?" "Yes, Little Bird, you can be a fireman. You can be anything you put your mind to."

Later that night in bed, Little Bird said,
"Mom, Dad, I want to be a pirate who
sails on the high seas!" "Yes, Little Bird,
you can be anything you want to be —

like those two guys over there who wanted their own Tiki Hut in the middle of nowhere. They made their dream come true!" Little Bird said, "Tomorrow I am telling all my friends."

"Okay, good night Little Bird."

ittle Bird was very excited the next
morning. He brushed his beak, made his
bed, and had his breakfast. He went to his
friend Junior's house. Junior was an octopus.
"Junior, I am going to be a pirate."

Mr. Octopus said, "You can't be a pirate
Little Bird. Stick to being a little bird. That's
what you're supposed to be."

Little Bird said, "You watch! I will be a pirate. I will!" Junior said, "Well, I am going to be a legendary octopus someday!"

Junior's mom replies, "Well first Mr. Legendary, let's try and find all your shoes!"

Little Bird went to Edgar Crab's house and said, "I am going to be a pirate!" "Ha ha ha ha ha!" Papa Crab laughed. "That's a nice dream, Little Bird, but you're too small. Birds can't be pirates anyway." "Yes they can! I would work for crackers to be a pirate!"

Little Edgar said, "Ha ha! You would have to be half crackers to want to be a pirate, Little Bird." "You're wrong. I will show you!

"Boy oh boy, those guys are crabby," Little Bird said as he left to find another friend.

ittle Bird went to Baby Keith's house. Baby Keith was a walrus who lived with his mother, father, and grandparents. "I am going to be a pirate!" Little Bird said.

"You can't be a pirate. You're a bird, and you're just too little." Baby Keith asked his Grandpa, "Can I be a pirate too?"

Grandpa said, "Don't even think about it, Baby Keith. You are going to be a famous walrus chef someday. Now, Little Bird, go home and stop talking all this pirate nonsense." Little Bird said, "You're wrong. I will show you!"

ittle Bird went to see his friend Jake
Otter. Little Bird said, "Guess what?
I am going to be a pirate who sails the high
seas on a big pirate ship!"

Jake said, "I want to be a pirate too, mom."
Mrs. Otter said, "Now wait a minute Jake.
You're staying in otter school. There is no
otter choice for you young man!"
So, Little Bird left to tell more friends.

ittle Bird went to his friend Sig's house.
Sig was a starfish who lived with his
family. "Sig! I am going to be a pirate!" said
Little Bird. Little Sig said, "I want to be a
pirate too. That sounds like fun!"

Sig's mom said, "You could both be pirates!

You can be anything you put your mind to. Like my sister, who was a star on the walk of fame on Hollywood Boulevard. She got tired of people walking all over her, though."

Uncle Sheriff Starfish said, "I saw a pirate ship on the horizon. You should go talk to them."

Little Bird wasn't the best flyer, but he flew all day as fast as he could to catch the pirate ship.

A big storm blew in, but that didn't stop Little Bird. He flew and flew. The wind blew him around, and his wings were tired.

He had to catch that ship. It was his only chance. He was going to be a pirate!

The next morning the storm was gone. Little Bird finally caught up with the pirate ship. "Ahoy," he called to the ship. "I had to fly all day and night through a storm to catch you!

I want to be a pirate! I am honest, and I will work hard!"

The crew on board the BANDIT was the great pirate Captain Don Task, Crazy Eyes, Scratches the Cat and Buddy the Dog. "Aarghh!" Captain Don Task said. "Did you fly through the storm to get here?" "Yes, all night," said Little Bird. "Anyone who does that deserves a chance to be a pirate," said the Captain. "But it's a lot of hard work. You have to earn the respect of the crew. Then, and only then, you can be a pirate.

Come on aboard if you are ready." Little Bird says, "Squawk! Squawk! That's a yes!"

Captain Don Task appointed Crazy Eyes to show Little Bird all the things he needed to learn to be a pirate. Crazy Eyes was the best look out there was. He showed Little Bird how to look for rocks, other ships, and land.

Crazy Eyes had a
lot of stories
about the boat.
"Aarghh," he said.
"We once had a monkey
on here who went bananas,
and an elephant who
worked for peanuts.
"If you work hard, you
can earn a place on the ship.
The captain will give you a
pirate hat. Then you will
be a real pirate." "Well,
I am ready to go
to work," said
Little Bird.

He did all of his watches!

He swabbed the decks!

Being a pirate isn't easy. Pirates have so many chores to do! Wake up and make the bed. Then, there is breakfast to be made, raise the main sails, swab the decks, be on look out watches, lower the main sails, then swab the decks again, and then it's time to make dinner.

Because Little Bird was such a good worker, the Captain pulled him aside one evening and said, "Aarghh!

We want you to stay on and be a pirate with us." Then he gave Little Bird a pirate hat. Little Bird said, "Yippee! Thank you, Captain! Aarghh! Squawk!" He was a real pirate now.

The ship was running low on supplies so Captain Don Task ordered the crew to, "Raise the main sail! We are headed to town!" Little Bird was so very excited to get home and tell his friends and family that he was a REAL LIVE PIRATE.

When they arrived in town, all of Little Bird's friends were waiting at the dock. Sig Starfish, Junior Octopus, Edgar Crab, Keith Walrus, and Jake Otter were all waving and cheering, "Hurray! Hurray!"

"Mom. Dad. I did it! Aarghh! I am a pirate!" Papa Bird said, "We always knew you could, son. It doesn't matter what anyone says. If you work hard, and put your mind to it you can

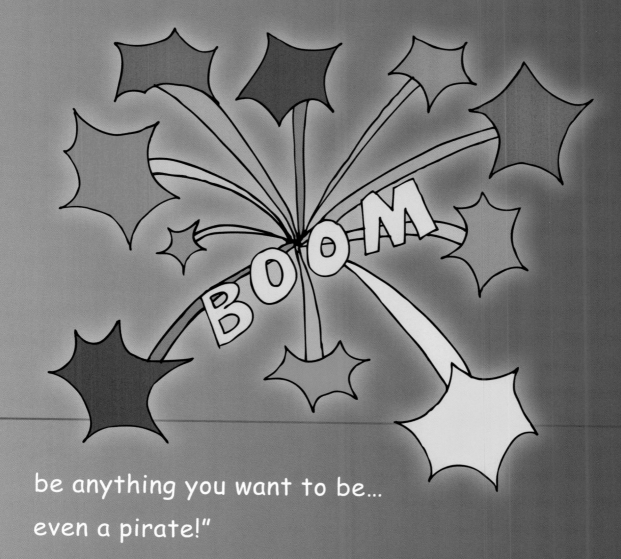

be anything you want to be...
even a pirate!"

Captain Don Task and Crazy Eyes set off
fireworks for a good old pirate celebration.

There would be many more adventures
ahead for Little Bird.

The End!

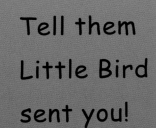

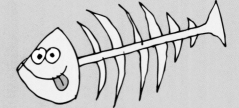